by Pearl Markovics

Consultant:
Beth Gambro
Reading Specialist
Yorkville, Illinois

Contents

BEARPORT PUBLISHING

New York, New York

Frog Log

Let's rhyme!

Here is a **dog**.

The small **dog** goes for a **jog**.

He sees a fat **hog**.

Then, the sky
fills with **fog**.

The **hog** finds a **bog**.

Then, the **dog** spots a **frog**!

"Ribbit!" says the **frog** on a **log**.

Key Words in the **-og** Family

bog　　**dog**　　**fog**　　**frog**

hog　　**jog**　　**log**

Other **-og** Words: **blog, cog, slog, smog**

Index

About the Author

Pearl Markovics enjoys having fun with words. She especially likes witty wordplay.

Teaching Tips

Before Reading

✔ Introduce rhyming words and the **–og** word family to readers.

✔ Guide readers on a "picture walk" through the text by asking them to name the things shown.

✔ Discuss book structure by showing children where text will appear consistently on pages. Highlight the supportive pattern of the book.

During Reading

✔ Encourage readers to "read with your finger" and point to each word as it is read. Stop periodically to ask children to point to a specific word in the text.

✔ Reading strategies: When encountering unknown words, prompt readers with encouraging cues such as:

   • **Does that word look like a word you already know?**
   • **Does it rhyme with another word you have already read?**

After Reading

✔ Write the key words on index cards.

   • **Have readers match them to pictures in the book.**

✔ Ask readers to identify their favorite page in the book. Have them read that page aloud.

✔ Choose an **–og** word. Ask children to pick a word that rhymes with it.

✔ Ask children to create their own rhymes using **–og** words. Encourage them to use the same pattern found in the book.

Credits: Cover, © LifetimeStock/Shutterstock and © josefauer/Shutterstock; 2, © Africa Studio/Shutterstock; 2–3, © Odua Images/Shutterstock and © Richard Peterson/Shutterstock; 4–5, © Bigandt.com/Shutterstock; 6–7, © Eric Isselee/Shutterstock; 8, © Ouda Images/Shutterstock; 9, © Eric Isselee/Shutterstock; 8–9, © alicija neumiler/Shutterstock; 10–11, © jadimages/Shutterstock; 12, © MirasWonderland/Shutterstock; 12–13, © LifetimeStock/Shutterstock and © josefauer/Shutterstock; 14–15, © LifetimeStock/Shutterstock, © josefauer/Shutterstock, and © Jagodka/Shutterstock; 16T (L to R), © Patrick Tr/Shutterstock, © Odua Images/Shutterstock, © alicija neumiler/Shutterstock, and © LifetimeStock/Shutterstock; 16B (L to R), © Eric Isselee/Shutterstock, © Bigandt.com/Shutterstock, and © josefauer/Shutterstock.

Publisher: Kenn Goin   **Senior Editor**: Joyce Tavolacci   **Creative Director**: Spencer Brinker

Library of Congress Cataloging-in-Publication Data: Names: Markovics, Pearl, author. | Gambro, Beth, consultant. Title: Frog log / by Pearl Markovics; consultant: Beth Gambro, Reading Specialist, Yorkville, Illinois. Description: New York, New York: Bearport Publishing, [2020] | Series: Read and rhyme: Level 2 | Includes index. Identifiers: LCCN 2019007616 (print) | LCCN 2019012643 (ebook) | ISBN 9781642806076 (ebook) | ISBN 9781642805536 (library) | ISBN 9781642807110 (pbk.) Subjects: LCSH: Readers (Primary) Classification: LCC PE1119 (ebook) | LCC PE1119 .M28536 2020 (print) | DDC 428.6/2—dc23 LC record available at https://lccn.loc.gov/2019007616

10 9 8 7 6 5 4 3 2 1